It was a young brown bear and his name was Douglas. 'I NEED A HUG,' said Douglas.

So he wriggled
out of his pyjamas,

brushed his hair,

put on a scarf and went to look for one.

'My best hugs are BIG,' thought Douglas so he went up to the biggest thing he could find, wrapped his arms all the way around

and gave it a
squeeze.
It didn't feel quite
right.

'Oooh!' grunted Douglas.
'It's a bit too...

...heavy!'

'My best hugs are **TALL**,' thought Douglas.
So he went up to the tallest thing he could find.

He hugged
the bottom...

he hugged around
the middle...

and he hugged as high as he could reach. But it was all wrong. And it had splinters.

'My best hugs are comfy,' thought Douglas and he trotted towards a cosy-looking bush.

He cuddled the bush but something felt very odd.
The leaves quivered and trembled...

...and ran away!

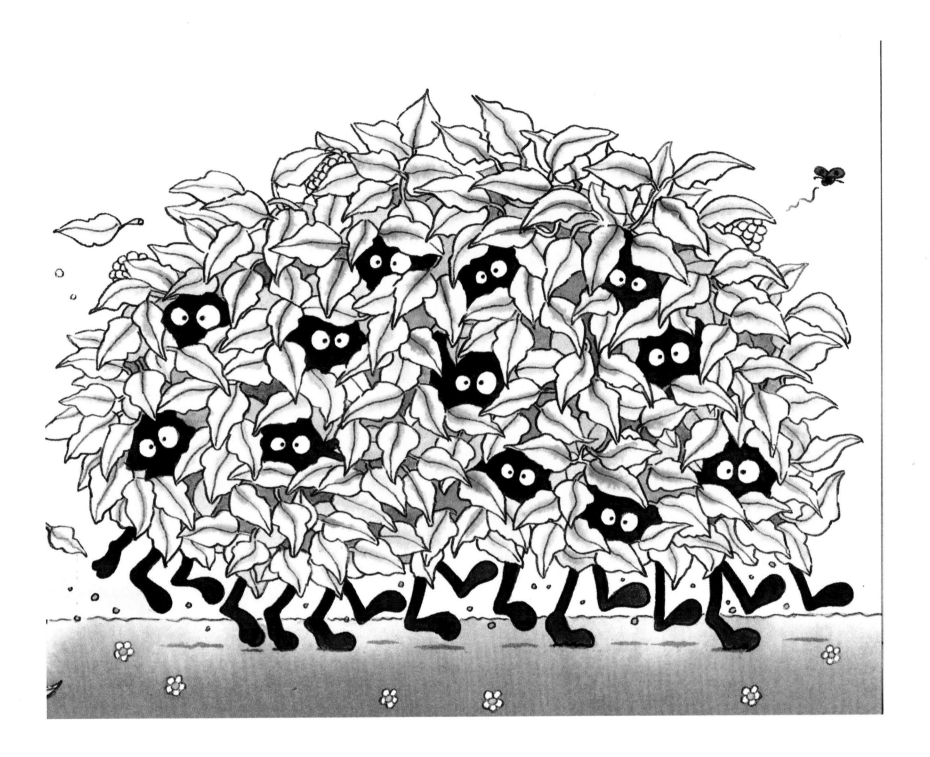

'GIVE US A HUG!'
cried Douglas.

'No!' baa-ed the sheep,
'we're too busy.'
He scooped up
armfuls anyway

and tried to cuddle
them gently,
but they kicked and
squirmed and didn't
like it at all.

Poor Douglas!
'WHY CAN'T I FIND
A HUG?' he said.
'If I want a hug,'
said a wise owl,
'I sit in my tree
and-'

'Let me try!'
whooped Douglas
and he scrambled
up next to the owl.

But he soon found himself in a clumsy muddle.

'Twooooooooo Twit!' said the owl crossly.

He felt something long-eared and rabbity and gave it a tug. Douglas could tell the rabbit didn't want a hug.

'I only wanted a hug,' sniffed Douglas. 'Perhaps there's one down here?'

'BUT I NEED A HUG,'
said Douglas,
'and I can't find
one anywhere.'

He sniffed again and, without thinking, wiped his nose on the fluffy end.

'Exscuuuuse me!' shouted the rabbit. 'Put me down!'

'Oh, I see,' said the rabbit kindly. 'Come with me.'

He took Douglas
by the paw...
...and led him round
and about.

At last they came to a deep dark cave where a sleepy someone was just waking up.

Douglas peeped inside. He had the funniest feeling that he knew the someone very well.

'HUG?' asked Douglas, and ran as fast as he could towards...

...his MUM! "Come to think of it, my best hugs are from someone I love,' said Douglas. And he snuggled into

the biggest,
warmest arms
he knew.

Sandwich Hug

Goodnight Hug

Upside-Down Hug

Don't-let-Go Hug

Falling Hug

Shy Hug

Group Hug

Back-to-Front Hug

Solo Hug

Tummy Hug

Daisy-Chain Hug

Big Hug

Come-and- Get-it Hug

Unrequited Hug

THE END

HUGLESS DOUGLAS

DAVID MELLING

525 684 31 2

One spring morning a big yaaawwwwn came from the back of a deep dark cave.